These levels are meant only as guides,
you and your child can best choose a book that's right.

Level 1: Kindergarten–Grade 1 . . . Ages 4–6
- word bank to highlight new words
- consistent placement of text to promote readability
- easy words and phrases
- simple sentences build to make simple stories
- art and design help new readers decode text

Level 2: Grade 1 . . . Ages 6–7
- word bank to highlight new words
- rhyming texts introduced
- more difficult words, but vocabulary is still limited
- longer sentences and longer stories
- designed for easy readability

Level 3: Grade 2 . . . Ages 7–8
- richer vocabulary of up to 200 different words
- varied sentence structure
- high-interest stories with longer plots
- designed to promote independent reading

Level 4: Grades 3 and up . . . Ages 8 and up
- richer vocabulary of more than 300 different words
- short chapters, multiple stories, or poems
- more complex plots for the newly independent reader
- emphasis on reading for meaning

LEVEL 4

Library of Congress Cataloging-in-Publication Data Available

2 4 6 8 10 9 7 5 3 1

Published by Sterling Publishing Co., Inc.
387 Park Avenue South, New York, NY 10016
Text © 2006 by Harriet Ziefert Inc.
Illustrations © 2006 by Deborah Zemke
Distributed in Canada by Sterling Publishing
c/o Canadian Manda Group, 165 Dufferin Street,
Toronto, Ontario, Canada M6K 3H6
Distributed in the United Kingdom by GMC Distribution Services,
Castle Place, 166 High Street, Lewes, East Sussex, England BN7 1XU
Distributed in Australia by Capricorn Link (Australia) Pty. Ltd.
P.O. Box 704, Windsor, NSW 2756, Australia

I'm Going To Read is a trademark of Sterling Publishing Co., Inc.

Sterling ISBN-13: 978-1-4027-3429-8
ISBN-10: 1-4027-3429-8

For information about custom editions, special sales, premium and
corporate purchases, please contact Sterling Special Sales
Department at 800-805-5489 or specialsales@sterlingpub.com.

DON'T
FEED THE
BABYSITTER
TO YOUR
BOA
CONSTRICTOR

43 RIDICULOUS RULES
EVERY KID SHOULD KNOW!

Deborah Zemke

Sterling Publishing Co., Inc.
New York

INTRODUCTION

You already know all the important rules.
You look both ways before you cross the
street. You raise your hand in class.
You always tell your mother how much
you appreciate everything she does for
you and how good she looks even when
it's five o'clock in the morning and
you're practicing your trumpet.

You already know when to walk,
not walk, sit, stand, and talk. You know
when to say "please" and when to say
"cheese." Now it's time to learn some
rules that are so ridiculous you will
never need to follow them.

Chapter 1
EATING

Never eat spaghetti
through your nose.

RULE NO. 2

You may eat your food with your fingers,
but you must never eat your fingers
with your food.

RULE NO. 3

Never eat anything that
is still moving.

Don't cut your meat
with scissors.

RULE NO. 5

Be a member of the
Clean Plate Club.
Eat your food directly
from the table.

RULE NO. 6

Don't eat your cereal from the fishbowl.

RULE NO. 7

Insist on eating carrots
at every meal until your
skin turns orange.

RULE NO. 8

Do not eat with your feet, nose,
bottom, knees, chest, forehead,
or ears on the table.

RULE NO. 9

Chew your food only once or twice
before swallowing.

Ask your mother to install
a drive-through window in the kitchen.

RULE NO. 11

Don't make mountains out of
your mashed potatoes.

RULE NO. 12

Drink at least four glasses of milk,
three glasses of orange juice,
and ten glasses of water every day.

RULE NO. 13

Be realistic about dinner.
It's not always going to be pizza and potato
chips. It's not always going to be good.

What to Do with Food You Simply Cannot Eat

b) Feed it to the dog.

a) Mash it with your fork
   until it can't be recognized.

d) Stick it
   under the table.

c) Feed it to the baby.

Order peanut-butter-and-jelly
sandwiches on white bread, no crust—
even in Chinese restaurants.

How to Eat a Sandwich with Chopsticks

You can hold
two chopsticks
in one hand . . .

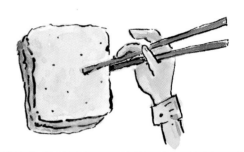

one chopstick
in each hand . . .

or one chopstick
in two hands!

Chapter 2

BROTHERS, SISTERS, PETS

RULE NO. 15

Do not bring your hamster to dinner.

RULE NO. 16

Don't decorate
the Christmas tree with
your sister's underwear.

Never send
your little brother
anywhere by mail.
It's too slow.

Don't feed the babysitter to your boa constrictor.

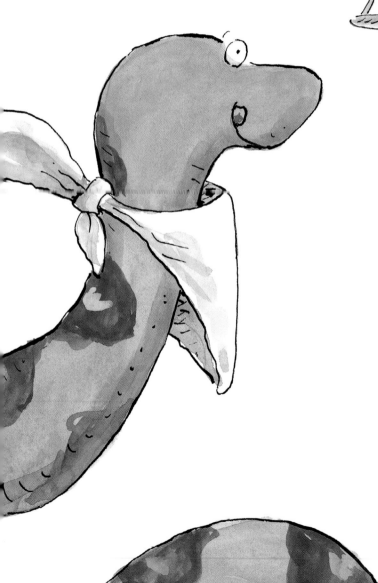

RULE NO. 19

Don't feed
your boa constrictor
to the babysitter.

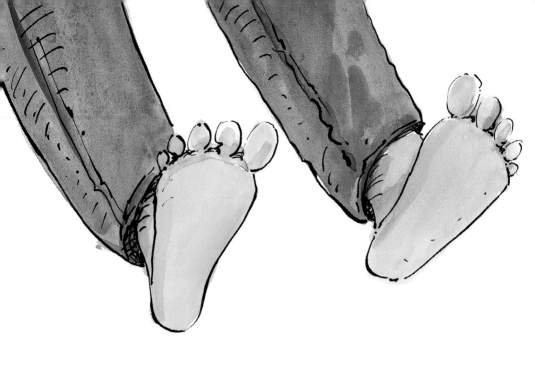

RULE NO. 20

Don't jump on the bed,
the couch, the chair, the car,
or the salamander.

RULE NO. 21

Never give
a cat a haircut unless
she asks for one.

RULE NO. 22

And never give
your sister a haircut—
even when she asks
for one.

Don't play Frisbee
with your dog at
the Grand Canyon.

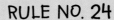

Don't make your
little brother count
to 5,000 while
you go hide.

Teach your dog
cool tricks.

Sit.

Roll over.

Fetch.

Fetch cookies and milk.

Teach your brother or
sister cool tricks.

Sit.

Roll over.

Fetch.

Fetch more
cookies and milk.

RULE NO. 27

Do not put a frog in your sister's bed.

Do not put your sister
in a frog's bed.

Penguins do not
make good pets, even if
you have a big freezer.

Chapter 3
YOUR PARENTS

RULE NO. 30

Never laugh at your father's tie
or your mother's hairstyle, even if they're
both yellow with green polka-dots.

Ask your mom and dad everything.

Why is the sky blue? Where do birds sleep? What is there to eat? Is there life on Mars? Can I take tuba lessons? Will you help me with my homework? Will you teach me how to do a handstand? Can I get a dog? Can I get a horse? Can I get a hippo? Can I stay over at Jimmy's house tonight? How do you get gum out of your hair? Why is there water dripping from the ceiling? Who was the 33rd president? How tall is a giraffe? What is the capital of Maryland? Why do I have to make my bed if I'm just going to unmake it again? What does 14 x 73 equal? Can I go watch TV? Can I grow a beard? Will you go bald like Grandpa? Why is Z the last letter of the alphabet? Can I change my name to Bruno?

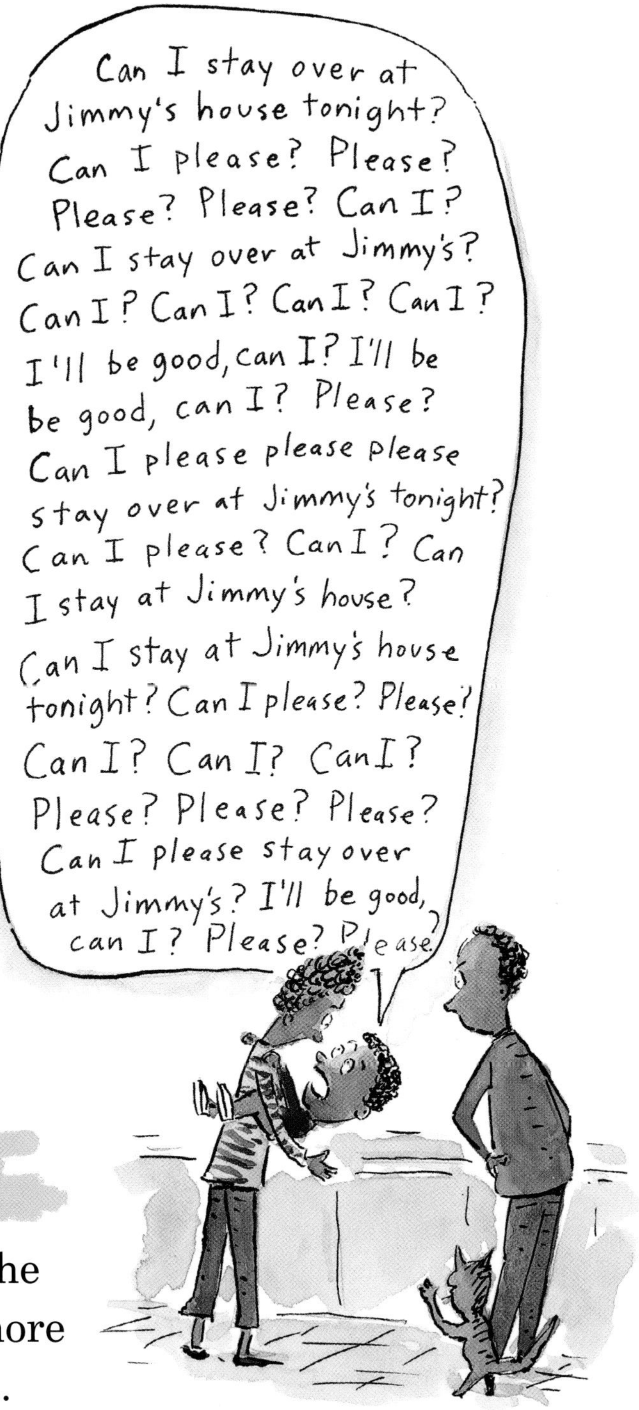

RULE NO. 32

But don't ask the same question more than 35 times.

RULE NO. 33

Be sure to bring
plenty of things to
keep you busy on
long car trips.

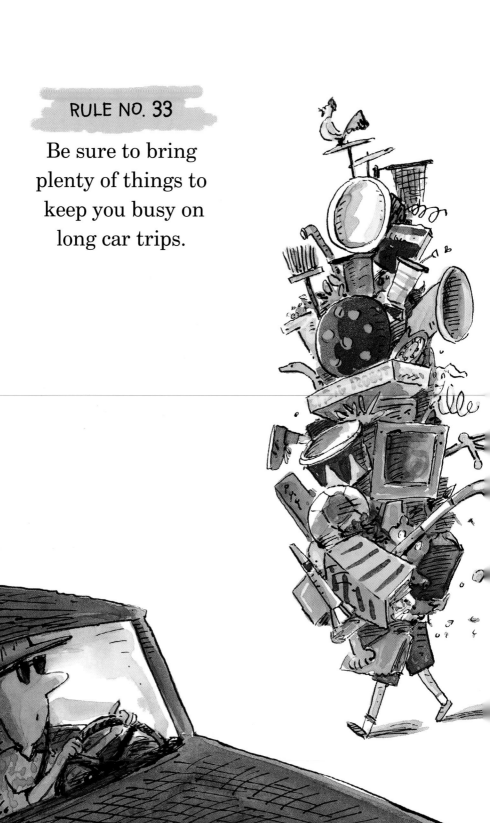

RULE NO. 34

Practice multiplication by always
asking for twice as much money
as you really need.

RULE NO. 35

If something in
your room starts growing,
tell your mother it's
a science project.

RULE NO. 36

If your socks stand up by themselves,
tell your father it's an art project.

Always remember your mother's birthday.
She will love anything you give her,
especially if you've made it yourself.

P.S. But don't give her
a worm necklace with matching earrings—
even if you dug up the worms yourself.

RULE NO. 38

In the car never ask,
"Are we there yet?"
Instead, ask over and over,
"Are you sure we're
going the right way?"

RULE NO. 39

Don't tell the new neighbors
that your mother is an alien.

RULE NO. 40

When your mother asks you to
take out the garbage, do not:

a) train the dog
to take it out
for you

b) put it in the
refrigerator

c) take it to the movies

One of the best ways to make
your mom and dad really proud
is to bring home a good report card.

Aeronautical Engineering A+

Physical Education A+

Oceanography A+

Communication Skills A+

Make your mother breakfast in bed.

RULE NO. 43

Read these rules first thing
every morning because there is
nothing better than starting your day
with a smile on your face.